This Book Belongs to

Ryan Walker

This Book Belongs to

Ryan Walker

MY BIG BOOK
OF RHYMES

ISBN 1-84135-134-2

Published by Award Publications Limited,
27 Longford Street, London NW1 3DZ

Printed in Singapore

MY BIG BOOK OF RHYMES

Illustrated by Lesley Smith

AWARD PUBLICATIONS LIMITED

The Mulberry Bush

Here we go round the mulberry bush,
The mulberry bush, the mulberry bush.
Here we go round the mulberry bush,
On a cold and frosty morning.

Who shall we send to fetch him out,
Fetch him out, fetch him out?
Who shall we send to fetch him out,
On a cold and frosty morning?

8

The Crooked Man

There was a crooked man,
And he walked a crooked mile.
He found a crooked sixpence
Beside a crooked stile.
He bought a crooked cat,
Which caught a crooked mouse,
And they all lived together
In a little crooked house.

Oranges and Lemons

Oranges and lemons,
Say the bells of St Clement's.

You owe me five farthings,
Say the bells of St Martin's.

When will you pay me?
Say the bells of Old Bailey.

When I grow rich,
Say the bells of Shoreditch.

When will that be?
Say the bells of Stepney.

I'm sure I don't know,
Says the great bell of Bow.

Here comes a candle to light you to bed,
Here comes a chopper to chop off your head.

11

Hey Diddle Diddle

Hey diddle diddle,
The cat and the fiddle,
The cow jumped over the moon;
The little dog laughed
To see such fun,
And the dish ran away with the spoon.

Old King Cole

Old King Cole was a merry old soul,
And a merry old soul was he.
He called for his pipe,
And he called for his bowl,
And he called for his fiddlers three.

Every fiddler, he had a fiddle,
And a very fine fiddle had he;
Oh, there's none so rare as can compare
With Old King Cole and his fiddlers three.

Daffy-down-dilly

Daffy-down-dilly is new come to town,
In a yellow petticoat, and a green gown.

Rain

Rain, rain, go away,
Come again another day.

Thirty Days Hath September

Thirty days hath September,
April, June, and November;
All the rest have thirty-one,
Excepting February alone,
And that has twenty-eight days clear
And twenty-nine in each leap year.

Sing a Song of Sixpence

Sing a song of sixpence,
A pocket full of rye;
Four and twenty blackbirds
Baked in a pie.

When the pie was opened,
The birds began to sing;
Wasn't that a dainty dish,
To set before the king?

The king was in his counting house,
Counting out his money;
The queen was in the garden,
Eating bread and honey.

The maid was in the garden,
Hanging out the clothes;
When down came a blackbird,
And pecked off her nose.

Hickory, Dickory, Dock

Hickory, dickory, dock,
The mouse ran up the clock.
The clock struck one,
The mouse ran down,
Hickory, dickory, dock.

Pussy Cat, Pussy Cat

Pussy cat, pussy cat,
Where have you been?
I've been up to London
To look at the Queen.
Pussy cat, pussy cat,
What did you there?
I frightened a little mouse
Under her chair.

18

Cock-a-doodle-doo!

Cock-a-doodle-doo!
My dame has lost her shoe,
My master's lost his fiddling stick,
And doesn't know what to do.

Higgledy, Piggledy

Higgledy, piggledy, my black hen,
She lays eggs for gentlemen.
Sometimes nine and sometimes ten,
Higgledy, piggledy, my black hen.

One, Two, Buckle My Shoe

One, two,
Buckle my shoe;
Three, four,
Knock at the door;
Five, six,
Pick up sticks;
Seven, eight,
Lay them straight;
Nine, ten,
A big fat hen;
Eleven, twelve,
Dig and delve;
Thirteen, fourteen,
Maids a-courting;
Fifteen, sixteen,
Maids in the kitchen;
Seventeen, eighteen,
Maids in waiting;
Nineteen, twenty,
My plate's empty.

Rock-a-bye Baby

Rock-a-bye baby,
On the tree-top.
When the wind blows
The cradle will rock.

When the bough breaks,
The cradle will fall.
Down will come baby,
Cradle and all.

Little Miss Muffet

Little Miss Muffet
Sat on a tuffet,
Eating her curds and whey;
There came a big spider,
Who sat down beside her
And frightened Miss Muffet
away.

Simple Simon

Simple Simon met a pieman,
Going to the fair;
Says Simple Simon to the pieman,
Let me taste your ware.

Says the pieman to Simple Simon,
Show me first your penny;
Says Simple Simon to the pieman,
Indeed I have not any.

Cobbler, Cobbler

Cobbler, cobbler, mend my shoe,
Get it done by half past two;
Stitch it up and stitch it down,
Then I'll give you half a crown.

If I Had as Much Money

If I had as much money as I could spend,
I never would cry, old chairs to mend!
Old chairs to mend! Old chairs to mend!
I never would cry, old chairs to mend!

If I had as much money as I could tell,
I never would cry, old clothes to sell!
Old clothes to sell! Old clothes to sell!
I never would cry, old clothes to sell!

Monday's Child

Monday's child
  is fair of face,
Tuesday's child
  is full of grace.
Wednesday's child
  is full of woe.
Thursday's child
  has far to go.
Friday's child
  is loving and giving,
Saturday's child
  works hard for a living.
But the child that is born
  on the Sabbath day
Is bonny and blithe,
  and good and gay.

Incey Wincey Spider

Incey Wincey spider
Climbing up the spout;
Down came the rain
And washed the spider out;
Out came the sun
And dried out all the rain;
Incey Wincey spider
Climbed up the spout again.

Doctor Foster

Doctor Foster went to Gloucester
In a shower of rain;
He stepped in a puddle,
Right up to his middle,
And never went there again.

The Milk Maid

Where are you going to, my pretty maid?
I'm going a-milking, sir, she said,
Sir, she said, sir, she said,
I'm going a-milking, sir, she said.

May I go with you, my pretty maid?
You're kindly welcome, sir, she said,
Sir, she said, sir, she said,
You're kindly welcome, sir, she said.

Say, will you marry me, my pretty maid?
Yes, if you please, kind sir, she said,
Sir, she said, sir, she said,
Yes, if you please, kind sir, she said.

What is your father, my pretty maid?
My father's a farmer, sir, she said,
Sir, she said, sir, she said,
My father's a farmer, sir, she said.

What is your fortune, my pretty maid?
My face is my fortune, sir, she said,
Sir, she said, sir, she said,
My face is my fortune, sir, she said.

Then I can't marry you, my pretty maid.
Nobody asked you, sir, she said,
Sir, she said, sir, she said,
Nobody asked you, sir, she said.

Two Little Dicky-birds

Two little dicky-birds
Sitting on a wall,
One named Peter, one named Paul,
Fly away Peter, fly away Paul;
Come back Peter,
Come back Paul.

Beg Pardon, Mrs Hardin

Beg pardon, Mrs Hardin,
Is my kitty in your garden?
Yes she is, and all alone,
Chewing on a mutton bone.

To Bed, to Bed

To bed, to bed, said Sleepy-head.
Tarry a while, said Slow.
Put on the pan, said Greedy Ann,
We'll sup before we go.

28

Twinkle, Twinkle, Little Star

Twinkle, twinkle, little star,
How I wonder what you are!
Up above the world so high,
Like a diamond in the sky.

Wee Willie Winkie

Wee Willie Winkie runs through the town,
Upstairs and downstairs, in his nightgown,
Rapping at the window, crying through the lock:
Are the children in their beds, for it's past eight o'clock?

London Bridge

London Bridge is falling down,
Falling down, falling down.
London Bridge is falling down,
My fair lady.

Build it up with iron bars,
Iron bars, iron bars.
Build it up with iron bars,
My fair lady.

Iron bars will bend and break,
Bend and break, bend and break.
Iron bars will bend and break,
My fair lady.

Build it up with silver and gold,
Silver and gold, silver and gold.
Build it up with silver and gold,
My fair lady.

Silver and gold I've not got,
I've not got, I've not got.
Silver and gold I've not got,
My fair lady.

Then off to prison you must go,
You must go, you must go.
Then off to prison you must go,
My fair lady.

As I Was Going to St Ives

As I was going to St Ives,
I met a man with seven wives;
Each wife had seven sacks,
Each sack had seven cats,
Each cat had seven kits:
Kits, cats, sacks and wives,
How many were there going to St Ives?

There Was a Little Girl

There was a little girl, and she had a little curl
Right in the middle of her forehead;
When she was good she was very, very good,
But when she was bad she was horrid.

Little Polly Flinders

Little Polly Flinders
Sat amongst the cinders,
Warming her pretty little toes;
Her mother came and caught her,
And whipped her little daughter
For spoiling her nice new clothes.

The Queen of Hearts

The Queen of Hearts
She made some tarts,
All on a summer's day;
The Knave of Hearts
He stole those tarts,
And took them clean away.

The Grand Old Duke of York

Oh, the grand old Duke of York,
He had ten thousand men;
He marched them up to the top of the hill,
And he marched them down again.
And when they were up, they were up,
And when they were down, they were down,
And when they were only half way up,
They were neither up nor down.

Humpty Dumpty

Humpty Dumpty sat on a wall,
Humpty Dumpty had a great fall;
All the king's horses and all the king's men
Couldn't put Humpty together again.

35

This Little Pig

This little pig went to market,
This little pig stayed home,
This little pig had roast beef,
This little pig had none,
And this little pig cried,
Wee-wee-wee-wee-wee,
I can't find my way home.

36

Solomon Grundy

Solomon Grundy,
Born on a Monday,
Christened on Tuesday,
Married on Wednesday,
Took ill on Thursday,
Worse on Friday,
Died on Saturday,
Buried on Sunday.
That is the end
Of Solomon Grundy.

The House That Jack Built

This is the farmer sowing his corn,
That kept the cock that crowed in the morn,
That waked the priest all shaven and shorn,
That married the man all tattered and torn,
That kissed the maiden all forlorn,
That milked the cow with the crumpled horn,
That tossed the dog,
That worried the cat,
That killed the rat,
That ate the malt
That lay in the house that Jack built.

Six Little Mice Sat Down to Spin

Six little mice sat down to spin;
Pussy passed by and she peeped in.
What are you doing, my little men?
Weaving coats for gentlemen.
Shall I come and cut off your threads?
No, no, Mistress Pussy, you'd bite off our heads.
Oh, no, I'll not; I'll help you to spin.
That may be so, but you don't come in.

Ride a Cock-horse

Ride a cock-horse to Banbury Cross,
To see a fine lady upon a white horse;
With rings on her fingers and bells on her toes,
She shall have music wherever she goes.

Tom He Was a Piper's Son

Tom he was a piper's son,
He learnt to play when he was young,
And all the tune that he could play
Was, Over the Hills and Far Away.
Over the hills and a great way off,
The wind shall blow my top-knot off.

Tom with his pipe made such a noise
That he pleased both the girls and boys,
And they stopped to hear him play,
Over the Hills and Far Away.

Tom with his pipe did play with such skill
That those who heard him could never keep still;
As soon as he played they began for to dance,
Even pigs on their hind legs would after him prance.

Little Tommy Tucker

Little Tommy Tucker
Sings for his supper:
What shall we give him?
White bread and butter.
How shall he cut it
Without e'er a knife?
How will he be married
Without e'er a wife?

Pease Porridge

Pease porridge hot, pease porridge cold,
Pease porridge in the pot, nine days old.
Some like it hot, some like it cold,
Some like it in the pot, nine days old.

Curly Locks

Curly locks, Curly locks, wilt thou be mine?
Thou shalt not wash dishes, nor yet feed the swine,
But sit on a cushion and sew a fine seam,
And feed upon strawberries, sugar and cream.

Three Blind Mice

Three blind mice,
See how they run!
They all ran after the farmer's wife,
Who cut off their tails with a carving knife,
Did you ever see such a thing in your life,
As three blind mice?

Baa, Baa, Black Sheep

Baa, baa, black sheep,
Have you any wool?
Yes, sir, yes, sir,
Three bags full;
One for the master,
And one for the dame,
And one for the little boy
Who lives down the lane.

Little Bo-peep

Little Bo-peep has lost her sheep,
And doesn't know where to find them;
Leave them alone, and they'll come home,
Bringing their tails behind them.

Ding, Dong, Bell

Ding, dong, bell,
Pussy's in the well.
Who put her in?
Little Johnny Green.
Who pulled her out?
Little Tommy Stout.
What a naughty boy was that
To try to drown poor pussy cat,
Who never did him any harm,
And killed all the mice in the farmer's barn.

See-saw, Margery Daw

See-saw, Margery Daw,
Jacky shall have a new master;
Jacky shall have but a penny a day,
Because he can't work any faster.

Georgie Porgie

Georgie Porgie, pudding and pie,
Kissed the girls and made them cry;
When the boys came out to play,
Georgie Porgie ran away.

I Had a Little Pony

I had a little pony,
His name was Dapple Grey;
I lent him to a lady
To ride a mile away.
She whipped him, she slashed him,
She rode him through the mire;
I would not lend my pony now,
For all the lady's hire.

How Many Miles to Babylon?

How many miles to Babylon?
Three-score miles and ten.
Can I get there by candle-light?
Yes, and back again.
If your heels are nimble and light,
You may get there by candle-light.

See-saw, Sacradown

See-saw, Sacradown,
Which is the way to London Town?
One foot up, the other foot down,
That is the way to London Town.

I Saw a Ship A-sailing

I saw a ship a-sailing,
A-sailing on the sea,
And oh, but it was laden
With pretty things for thee!

There were comfits in the cabin,
And apples in the hold;
The sails were made of silk,
And the masts were all of gold.

The four-and-twenty sailors
That stood between the decks,
Were four-and-twenty white mice
With chains about their necks.

The captain was a duck
With a packet on his back,
And when the ship began to move
The captain said, Quack! Quack!

Polly Put the Kettle On

Polly put the kettle on,
Polly put the kettle on,
Polly put the kettle on,
We'll all have tea.

Sukey take it off again,
Sukey take it off again,
Sukey take it off again,
They've all gone away.

I Love Little Pussy

I love little pussy,
Her coat is so warm,
And if I don't hurt her
She'll do me no harm.
So I'll not pull her tail,
Or drive her away,
But pussy and I
Very gently will play.
She shall sit by my side,
And I'll give her her food;
And pussy will love me
Because I am good.

Hot Cross Buns

Hot cross buns,
Hot cross buns,
One a penny, two a penny,
Hot cross buns!
If your daughters do not like them,
Give them to your sons.
One a penny, two a penny,
Hot cross buns!

Pat-a-cake

Pat-a-cake, pat-a-cake, baker's man,
Bake me a cake as fast as you can.
Pat it and prick it and mark it with B,
And put it in the oven for Baby and me.

There Was an Old Woman
Who Lived in a Shoe

There was an old woman who lived in a shoe,
She had so many children she didn't know what to do;
She gave them some broth without any bread;
She whipped them all soundly and sent them to bed.

56

Boys and Girls Come Out to Play

Boys and girls come out to play,
The moon doth shine as bright as day.
Leave your supper and leave your sleep,
And join your playfellows in the street.
Come with a whoop and come with a call,
Come with a good will or not at all.
Up the ladder and down the wall,
A half-penny loaf will serve us all;
You find milk and I'll find flour,
And we'll have a pudding in half an hour.

The Lion and the Unicorn

The lion and the unicorn
Were fighting for the crown;
The lion beat the unicorn
All around the town.
Some gave them white bread,
And some gave them brown;
Some gave them plum cake,
And drummed them out of town.

58

Old Mother Hubbard

Old Mother Hubbard
Went to the cupboard,
To fetch her poor dog a bone;
But when she got there
The cupboard was bare
And so the poor dog had none.

Jack Sprat

Jack Sprat could eat no fat,
His wife could eat no lean,
And so between them both, you see,
They licked the platter clean.

Jack ate all the lean,
Joan ate all the fat,
The bone, they picked it clean,
Then gave it to the cat.

Diddle, Diddle, Dumpling

Diddle, diddle, dumpling, my son John,
Went to bed with his trousers on;
One shoe off and one shoe on,
Diddle, diddle, dumpling, my son John.

It's Raining

It's raining, it's pouring,
The old man's snoring;
He went to bed
And bumped his head
And couldn't get up in the morning.

There Was an Old Woman Tossed Up in a Basket

There was a old woman tossed up in a basket,
Seventeen times as high as the moon;
Where she was going I couldn't but ask it,
For in her hand she carried a broom.

Old woman, old woman, old woman, quoth I,
Where are you going to up so high?
To brush the cobwebs off the sky!
May I go with you? Aye, by-and-by.

Mary, Mary, Quite Contrary

Mary, Mary, quite contrary,
How does your garden grow?
With silver bells and cockle shells,
And pretty maids all in a row.

Round and Round the Garden

Round and round the garden
Went the teddy bear,
One step,
Two steps,
Tickly under there.

Snail, Snail, Put Out Your Horns

Snail, snail, put out your horns
And I'll give you bread and barley corns.

Goosey Goosey Gander

Goosey goosey gander,
Whither shall I wander?
Upstairs and downstairs
And in my lady's chamber.
There I met an old man
Who would not say his prayers.
I took him by the left leg,
And threw him down the stairs.

Tom, Tom, the Piper's Son

Tom, Tom, the piper's son,
Stole a pig and away he run;
The pig was eat,
And Tom was beat,
And Tom went howling down
  the street.

Mary Had a Little Lamb

Mary had a little lamb,
Its fleece was white as snow
And everywhere that Mary went
The lamb was sure to go.

It followed her to school one day,
Which was against the rule;
It made the children laugh and play
To see a lamb at school.

One, Two, Three, Four, Five

One, two, three, four, five,
Once I caught a fish alive,
Six, seven, eight, nine, ten,
Then I let it go again.
Why did you let it go?
Because it bit my finger so.
Which finger did it bite?
This little finger on the right.

Dance To Your Daddy

Dance to your daddy,
My little babby,
Dance to your daddy, my little lamb;
You shall have a fishy
In a little dishy,
You shall have a fishy when the boat comes in.

Peter, Peter, Pumpkin Eater

Peter, Peter, pumpkin eater,
Had a wife and couldn't keep her;
He put her in a pumpkin shell
And there he kept her very well.

Round and Round the Rugged Rock

Round and round the rugged rock
The ragged rascal ran.
How many R's are there in that?
Now tell me if you can.

What Are Little Boys Made Of?

What are little boys made of, made of?
What are little boys made of?
Frogs and snails
And puppy-dogs' tails,
That's what little boys are made of.

What are little girls made of, made of?
What are little girls made of?
Sugar and spice
And all things nice,
That's what little girls are made of.

Ring o' Roses

Ring-a-ring o' roses,
A pocket full of posies,
A-tishoo! A-tishoo!
We all fall down.

Jack Be Nimble

Jack be nimble,
Jack be quick,
Jack jump over
The candlestick.

Jack and Jill

Jack and Jill
Went up the hill,
To fetch a pail of water;
Jack fell down,
And broke his crown,
And Jill came tumbling after.

Then up Jack got,
And home did trot,
As fast as he could caper;
He went to bed,
To mend his head
With vinegar and brown paper.

Do You Know the Muffin Man?

Oh do you know the muffin man,
The muffin man, the muffin man,
Oh do you know the muffin man,
Who lives in Drury Lane?

Oh yes, I know the muffin man,
The muffin man, the muffin man,
Oh yes, I know the muffin man,
Who lives in Drury Lane.

Lavender's Blue

Lavender's blue, dilly, dilly,
Lavender's green;
When I am king, dilly, dilly,
You shall be queen.

Call up your men, dilly, dilly,
Set them to work,
Some to the plough, dilly, dilly,
Some to the cart.

Some to make hay, dilly, dilly,
Some to thresh corn,
Whilst you and I, dilly, dilly,
Keep ourselves warm.

To Market, to Market

To market, to market,
To buy a fat pig;
Home again, home again,
Jiggety jig.

To market, to market,
To buy a fat hog;
Home again, home again,
Jiggety jog.

She Sells Sea-shells

She sells sea-shells on the sea shore;
The shells that she sells are sea-shells I'm sure.
So if she sells sea-shells on the sea shore,
I'm sure that the shells are sea-shore shells.

Pop! Goes the Weasel

Half a pound of tuppenny rice,
Half a pound of treacle,
Mix it up and make it nice,
Pop! goes the weasel.

Every night when I go out
The monkey's on the table;
Take a stick and knock it off,
Pop! goes the weasel.

Up and down the City Road,
In and out the Eagle,
That's the way the money goes,
Pop! goes the weasel.

A Frog He Would A-wooing Go

A frog he would a-wooing go,
Heigh ho! says Rowley,
A frog he would a-wooing go,
Whether his mother would let him or no.
With a rowley, powley, gammon and spinach
Heigh ho! says Anthony Rowley.

So off he set in his opera hat,
Heigh ho! says Rowley,
So off he set in his opera hat,
And on his way he met with a rat.
With a rowley, powley, gammon and spinach
Heigh ho! says Anthony Rowley.

Pray Mr Rat, will you go with me?
Heigh ho! says Rowley,
Pray Mr Rat, will you go with me?
Kind Mrs Mousey for to see?
With a rowley, powley, gammon and spinach
Heigh ho! says Anthony Rowley.

They came to the door of Mousey's hall,
Heigh ho! says Rowley,
They came to the door of Mousey's hall,
They gave a loud knock, and they gave a loud call.
With a rowley, powley, gammon and spinach
Heigh ho! says Anthony Rowley.

Pray, Mrs Mouse, are you within?
Heigh ho! says Rowley,
Pray, Mrs Mouse, are you within?
Oh yes, kind sirs, I'm sitting to spin,
With a rowley, powley, gammon and spinach.
Heigh ho! says Anthony Rowley.

Rub-a-dub-dub

Rub-a-dub-dub,
Three men in a tub,
And who do you think they be?
The butcher, the baker,
The candlestick-maker,
Turn them out, knaves all three!

Bobby Shafto

Bobby Shafto's gone to sea,
Silver buckles on his knee;
He'll come back and marry me,
Bonny Bobby Shafto.

Bobby Shafto's bright and fair,
Combing down his yellow hair,
He's my ain for evermair,
Bonny Bobby Shafto.

Little Boy Blue

Little Boy Blue,
Come blow your horn,
The sheep's in the meadow,
The cow's in the corn.

But where is the boy
Who looks after the sheep?
He's under the haystack,
Fast asleep.

Lucy Locket

Lucy Locket lost her pocket,
Kitty Fisher found it;
Not a penny was there in it,
Only ribbon round it.

One for Sorrow

One for sorrow,
Two for joy,
Three for a girl,
Four for a boy,
Five for silver,
Six for gold,
And seven for a secret
That's never been told.

Cross-patch

Cross-patch,
Draw the latch,
Sit by the fire and spin;
Take a cup,
And drink it up,
Then call your neighbours in.

I'm a Little Teapot

I'm a little teapot, short and stout;
Here's my handle, here's my spout.
When I see the tea-cups, hear me shout,
Tip me up and pour me out.

Three Wise Men of Gotham

Three wise men of Gotham,
They went to sea in a bowl,
And if the bowl had been stronger,
My song would have been longer.

I Saw Three Ships

I saw three ships come sailing by,
Sailing by, sailing by,
I saw three ships come sailing by,
On New Year's day in the morning.

And what do you think was in them then,
In them then, in them then?
And what do you think was in them then,
On New Year's day in the morning?

Three pretty girls were in them then,
In them then, in them then,
Three pretty girls were in them then,
On New Year's day in the morning.

And one could whistle, and one could sing,
And one could play on the violin,
Such joy there was at my wedding,
On New Year's day in the morning.

The Man in the Moon

The man in the moon
Came down too soon,
And asked the way to Norwich;
He went by the south,
And burnt his mouth
With supping cold plum porridge.

The North Wind Doth Blow

The north wind doth blow,
And we shall have snow,
And what will the robin do then,
Poor thing?
He'll sit in a barn,
And keep himself warm,
And hide his head under his wing,
Poor thing.

Peter Piper

Peter Piper picked a peck of pickled pepper;
A peck of pickled pepper Peter Piper picked.
If Peter Piper picked a peck of pickled pepper,
Where's the peck of pickled pepper Peter Piper picked?

If All the World

If all the world were apple-pie,
And all the seas were ink,
If all the trees were bread and cheese,
What should we do for drink?

Four and Twenty Tailors

Four and twenty tailors went to kill a snail,
The best man amongst them durst not touch her tail.
She put out her horns like a little Kyloe cow,
Run, tailors, run or she'll kill you all e'en now!

A Man in the Wilderness

A man in the wilderness asked of me
How many strawberries grew in the sea.
I answered him as I thought good,
As many red herrings as swim in the wood.

Please to Remember

Please to remember
The Fifth of November,
Gunpowder, treason and plot;
I see no reason
Why gunpowder treason
Should ever be forgot.

87

I Had a Little Nut Tree

I had a little nut tree,
Nothing would it bear
But a silver nutmeg
And a golden pear;
The King of Spain's daughter
Came to visit me,
And all for the sake
Of my little nut tree.

Index